This book belongs to:

_____

For Chris,
who only saw the
first draft and loved it.

This paperback edition first published in 2021 by Andersen Press Ltd.
First published in Great Britain in 2020 by Andersen Press Ltd.,
20 Vauxhall Bridge Road, London, SW1V 2SA
Copyright © Margaret Sturton 2020
The right of Margaret Sturton to be identified as the author and illustrator
of this work has been asserted by her in accordance with the
Copyright, Designs and Patents Act, 1988.

Printed and bound in China

1 3 5 7 9 10 8 6 4 2

British Cataloguing in Publication Data Available.
ISBN 978 1 78344 933 0
The Save the Children Fund is a charity registered in
England and Wales (213890) and Scotland (SC039570)

SAVE THE CHILDREN
Save the Children exists to help every child reach
their full potential. In the UK and around the
world, we make sure children keep safe, healthy and
learning, and change the future for good.

A Rabbit Called Herbert

(A Fox Called Herbert)

MARGARET STURTON

Andersen Press

Herbert loved foxes.

Herbert loved foxes so
much he made himself
a pair of red ears.

"Rabbit ears aren't short and pointy," laughed Herbert's mummy. Reluctantly, Herbert let his ears look rabbity again.

The next day, Herbert painted himself red
with the help of his little sister.

Then they played find-the-fox.

Herbert's mummy was cross.
"Look at the mess you've made!" she said.
"Promise me you will be a good rabbit."

Herbert helped to clean up.

A few days later, Herbert made himself a lovely new tail. He and his little sister played chase-a-tail until Mummy came to see what was happening.

"Cutting up my favourite dress was very naughty," scolded Herbert's mummy. "Promise me you will be a good rabbit."

Herbert said nothing.

Then, one day, when he was allowed out to play, Herbert did all the things he wasn't supposed to do.

He didn't try to be a good rabbit.

"Look, Mummy," said Herbert's little sister. "Look at Herbert."

"Herbert, come here, right away!"
called Herbert's mummy.

"I don't understand," said Herbert's mummy. "Why are you dressed like that when I asked you to be a good rabbit?"

"I CAN'T be a good rabbit!" said Herbert.
"Why not?" asked his mummy.
"Because..." said Herbert:

Herbert's mummy said
nothing as they looked
at each other.

Until, at last, she said,
"Oh Herbert...

Yes. You are my fox."